convivium

Time Piece

2021 Volume 6

Convivium 2021 Volume 6
Copyright © 2021 by Suzanne M. Lewis

Editor
Elisabeth Kramp

Cover Art
Cosmopolis Minor (detail), 2016, acrylic on canvas, Linnéa Gabriella Spransy

Layout
Joshua Stancil

Proofreader
Sara Harold

Publisher
Revolution of Tenderness

Contents

FROM THE EDITOR   6
Elisabeth Kramp

INTERVIEW
A Conversation With Classical Sculptor Thomas Marsh   8

POETRY

Mary Margaret Freeman
Empty House   15
Falling Upward *in the coronavirus pandemic*   18

Fred Dale
Come On Down   21

Greg Huteson
Apocalypse   36

Hannah Laurence
And the Needle Pulls   38
What Baboons We Are!   40

Michial Farmer
Holiday in Harlem   41

Will Stenberg
Divestments   42

Jane Greer
Glory in the Dead of Winter   46
Eine Kleine Nachtmusik   48

Andrew Calis
The Peace That Hides   61
The Voices in the Wind   62

Anna Key
Recompositions of Sonnets to Michelangelo by Vittoria
Colonna (No. 4, 19, 31, 41)   66

Elisabeth Kramp
A Larger Suit of Will   70

NONFICTION

Ewa Chrusciel
Louise Glück and the Return From Oblivion   50

Linnéa Gabriella Spransy
Artist Statement   64

FICTION

Pellegrine Deuel
Rondo   24

VISUAL ART

Thomas Marsh

Regina Coeli Christus Rex   10
Monument to Surfing   23
John the Baptist   47

Sharon Mollerus

Passing Time, Madrid Airport   17
Parking Mirror   35
Park Point, Duluth   39
Window Seat   45
IDS Center   54

Linnéa Gabriella Spransy

Parallelism   49
Solar Blush   69

CONTRIBUTORS   72

From the Editor

The phrase "gift of time" is popular in mindfulness practices, and, at its simplest, the idea is to reserve time to be with a loved one and to offer one's attention as the gift. It's interesting that we don't call this a "gift of attention," but instead place the emphasis on time itself. Perhaps we're aware that how we use our time often leaves our loved ones feeling like they don't have a share in our lives, our mortal measurement of time.

But if attention is key to loving our friends, family, and neighbors, how do we characterize this relationship between our time and our attention? This seems especially important to ask now, as many of us worry about having fractured or disordered attention.

We know that it takes time to cultivate attention, as in the case of learning how to identify birds or of learning how to read the work of a certain poet. Many of us have experienced improving our attention with practice: Whereas before we couldn't, now we're able to find pileated woodpeckers in the woods or are better equipped to consider a Les Murray poem in the context of his work.

Our theme for this issue of *Convivium* is "Time Piece," and we have here Thomas Marsh's thoughts on how a classical sculptor uses time, Ewa Chrusciel's discussion of the fallow and fertile periods in Louise Glück's poetry-writing life, and Linnéa Gabriella Spransy's observations about patterns that arise through time and space. The poets, fiction writers, and visual artists included in this issue have spent an unquantifiable number of hours, days, months, and years composing their work. In this way, their art is an opportunity for *convivenza*, a dwelling together by way of our mutual offerings of time and attention.

Elisabeth Kramp

A Conversation with Classical Sculptor Thomas Marsh

by Elisabeth Kramp

Thomas Marsh is a classical sculptor who has created many public monuments and has works in public and private collections throughout the United States. His noted works include the Monument to Surfing *in Santa Cruz, CA;* John the Baptist *at Mission San Juan Bautista, CA;* The Crucifix *and* Sanctuary *sculptures at St. Mary Catholic Church, Fredericksburg, VA; and* The Victims of Communism Memorial *(2007) in Washington, D.C. To see his work, please visit* http://thomasmarshsculptor.net.

On Monday, July 5, 2021, Thomas Marsh spoke with Convivium's *Elisabeth Kramp. The ensuing conversation has been edited for clarity and organized for ease of reading.*

Elisabeth: Thomas, how did you or others recognize your vocation, or gift, for a three-dimensional art, and how did you follow it?

Thomas: Overall, that recognition was indirect. I grew up in Sioux City, Iowa. Although there was quite an artistic tradition in architecture, in choral music—we know that Dvořák liked to come to Iowa in the summer—painting via Grant Wood, and a literary tradition that came from the University of Iowa Writers Workshop, there was little tradition in figurative sculpture. The visual arts in the region did include many design motifs from the Sioux Indians. Those Native American designs are remarkable and beautiful. "Down the river," in the Joslyn Art Museum in Omaha, Nebraska, has a great collection of works by the Sioux and other tribes in the area. I always felt that these were an influence on me that I couldn't have recognized at the time, the kind of design and compositional work that an artist picks up indirectly in childhood.

One inspiration I did consciously notice was the work of William Steele, a very fine Prairie School architect who designed the Woodbury County Courthouse in Sioux City. It's a 12-story building, a "Prairie School mini-skyscraper" dedicated in 1917. In the 1890's, Steele worked in the office of the great architect Louis Sullivan, as

Regina Coeli Christus Rex, Thomas Marsh

had Frank Lloyd Wright. The Woodbury County Courthouse had intensely magnificent figure sculptures by Alphonso Ianetti decorating two portals. These indeed were influences.

When I was eight years old, my older sister was a college student, minoring in art. She's 11 years older than me to the day, so we're like twins born 11 years apart. Well, I decided to play a prank on her when she modeled a clay medallion in the form of a large Roman coin, about 8 inches in diameter. I took some of her clay and re-created her medallion, and I switched her medallion with mine. It took years for her to believe that my sculpture was not in fact hers.

Elisabeth: Wow! They were that much alike that she didn't see the difference?

Thomas: Well, it took years for me to convince her that I'd switched the medallions!

Around that same time—about eight years old—I enjoyed making clay portrait heads, trying to make human likenesses. This was completely private and strictly for fun.

Because I was good at math and science, and because of the times—"space race"—there was pressure for students to go into those fields. I enrolled at Iowa State University right after high school in 1969, with the intention of becoming an architect. I quickly realized that there was only one field in which I had always had passion and gifts: representational art. I transferred to the Layton School of Art in Milwaukee, Wisconsin, and received a BFA in Painting in 1974.

I particularly enjoyed my anatomy studies at Layton, which allowed students to study and draw from cadavers at the Marquette University Medical School—the Medical College of Wisconsin. In fact, I asked for permission to spend more time studying from the cadavers. One of my professors said to me, *I think I can make a path for you.*

So, I ended up studying anatomy in the traditional way, gaining two med school credits by joining medical students in their mid-year anatomy studies there at the Medical College of Wisconsin.

Elisabeth: It looks like much of your sculptures are *living* bodies, but your work in morgues [the anatomy lab] must have helped you distinguish the body in life from the body in death.

Thomas: Yes, and it has especially affected what I do in portraiture.

I've written a mini-essay called "Portraiture and Personhood," which sketches the relationship of that "feeling of life" to one's relationship with God. Until Pope St. John Paul II gave us the term *personhood*, I found myself trying to explain this idea as "the experience of being alive," the experience of being a person.

I also have used the term "human spirit," which gets thrown around a lot now, to describe the experiential side of one's own being alive. It's not exactly the same as what psychologists call "the phenomenal self," but it's quite similar.

I'm a real fan of John Paul II's *Letter to Artists*, in which he addresses this idea of vocation—a calling.

Elisabeth: Yes, and he talks about the responsibility of answering that calling.

Thomas: Certainly. We know that in the parable of the talents, the servant who buried his master's money—literally, his *talents*—was admonished the harshest out of all the servants. What he did with the talents was the worst possible thing to do with them: nothing at all.

This idea of vocation, of a calling. I feel that if I did not do it, it would be morally wrong.

When I was 43, I met my bride-to-be, and we talked about this question of my calling as an artist and how it would affect my calling as a husband and father. I remember saying, "Those callings will not come into conflict with one another." And they haven't, by the grace of God.

Elisabeth: It sounds like time plays an important role in your life and work. Will you tell us a little about how you use time as a sculptor?

Thomas: I like this question about time. I think sculptors deal with time in at least five distinct contexts. First, we have long projects. A life-sized figure is about a year-long project. We know that our work is not going to be accomplished quickly.

I think the second is best described with a term I picked up from Apollo 8's moon mission in 1968, when it needed to make a "mid-course correction." In my work, there's always this possibility of making revisions; there's this progression as work comes into being, and sometimes it's important to make a mid-course correction.

Third... I'll call this one "dovetailing." One project takes multiple years, so I might work more or less concurrently on multiple projects without taking my mind off of the main one.

Fourth, sculpture is a very spatial art by its nature. It doesn't move. But it's a temporal process because it takes so long to complete. Eventually, a decision has to be made: Is it done, is it complete, is it finished? This makes me think of Michelangelo's *Slaves* in the Accademia in Florence: Are the works *finished*? In a sense they are, and in a sense they are not.

And, fifth, there's the experience of being disciplined as a visual artist in a way that requires flexibility. The unexpected happens—a bad casting, or materials that don't work the way one expected. I've heard writers talk about discipline in terms of needing to be at their desk a certain length of time per day. As a visual artist I have to be disciplined and flexible.

Elisabeth: And what is it like to see your work after it's installed?

Thomas: It's a very strange thing. I feel like a spectator, and it's an odd kind of feeling. Especially with my revisionist impulse, I might look at one of my public sculptures in frustration, trying to revise it in my mind. Because once it's installed, there's no way to revise! I had a wonderful painting teacher at Layton, Guido Brink, who said: *When you create these works, you have to let them go like they're your children who are leaving home.* That seems to be very true to the experience.

Empty House
by Mary Margaret Freeman

The little that I have
is really not a lot
but roll it round into a ball –
it looks the same as yours.

I trace snow–clad trees
on a breath–stained pane
toward a sky that's half–forgot.

I see your face reflected
there with mine
in that smudged and chalky
looking glass of us.

But in this house
– the secret twin of yours –
where some are gone
and the empty place is us

I hear - as from a shell
on another shore
beyond the clotted sea of sky –

    whispering

        assonances porous

 sibilants of presence

and I wonder –

Do you hear them too?

Passing Time, Madrid Airport, Sharon Mollerus

Falling Upward

in the coronavirus pandemic
by Mary Margaret Freeman

Here cabs and buses and thousands
quickened streets now stripped of clamor,
sirens wail, imprint our fears into the air.

Screens broadcast workers stacking
freezer trucks with bodies in zipper bags,
the rites of death overwhelmed,
the numbers of the dead ticking up,

reminding us though some
survive, too many are undone;
here is no forever
and goodbye too much never.

Yet *is* is stubborn too.

Here cabs and buses and thousands
quickened streets now stripped of clamor,
sirens wail, imprint our fears into the air.

Screens broadcast workers stacking
freezer trucks with bodies in zipper bags,
the rites of death overwhelmed,
the numbers of the dead ticking up,

reminding us though some
survive, too many are undone;
here is no forever
and goodbye too much never.

Yet *is* is stubborn too.
I plunge myself into its pool.

A patch of dirt and morning window sun
green a sprout of lettuce; a jasmine
sweet and starry overflows its pot.
With care, I tend and water both.

Midday a dove returns to
our smutted AC window ledge to peck
and dine on seeds and bits of fruit I strew.

Not a dirge his coo-roo-hoo
but a come-hither for his mate
to craft a twiggy careless place
for their clutch of two.

Lights winking on anticipate your ritual
return, of shedding clothes and shoes and gear

just inside the door – of all in getting clear –
for smiles, a kiss, hands to touch,
a talk, a table shared.

The gravity of the smallest things
pulls us out of the depths and like water wings
keep us buoyant in this drowning place.

To see them so is the path:
Falling upward we find the light.

Come On Down
by Fred Dale

It felt like the aircraft was cut loose from a 50 Ton Rotator
Tow Truck grinding up Pikes Peak, like the fatigued plane
was attempting to sit but misjudged distance to the chair,
maintained its freefall, catching traction at last, much later
than we thought it would, and continued on to New York.

This was weather's practice, as it turns out, for the micro-
burst that batted down Pan Am flight 759 into a neighbor-
hood of strong-roofed families, children hearing, before
anyone else, the return of their births. I had watched them
on the tarmac, the second plane queued up behind us, wai-

ting their turn to get underway, the port window portraits
of life's round charms inside. A boy like me, anticipating
the thunder of acceleration, a run at warp 10, like a metal
whale in an earthquake wave, the sharp jolts, the ship's b-

olts holding fast until the plane had nothing left to do, like any of us, but rise. For a moment, they must've felt what we felt, the focused shock of sinking beyond reason. And then that something different. The strike of the earth bell in a strong man's game. In Niagara Falls, I walked upstream, away from the barrel-breaking water, losing step-by-

step, the sleepless sound of crashing, to a place where the trees and bank-bound swirls forgave the urgency of the center, the forgetfulness of a future coming regardless, a hard lesson for a kid, or a river, each a conveyance for the grief we are likely to become.

Monument to Surfing, Thomas Marsh

Rondo
by Pellegrine Deuel

Beginning in December of 1889, a deadly virus surfaced in the Central Asian city of Bukhara (then part of the Russian empire). The outbreak swiftly traveled roads, railroad lines, and shipping routes to wipe out over a million people (out of a world population of 1.5 billion). Scientists hypothesize that the disease originated in cows. In addition to congestion, cough, fever, and intense fatigue, the sick experienced central nervous system symptoms, including loss of taste and smell. One patient, interviewed in a newspaper, described, "I felt as if I had been beaten with clubs for about an hour and then plunged into a bath of ice. My teeth chattered like castanets, and I consider myself lucky now to have gotten off with a whole tongue."[1] The virus attacked in waves, some of which were more lethal than the first.

Louise Michel, one of the original organizers of the Paris Commune, had gone on to become an infamous French agitator for the anarchist cause and was serving one of her numerous prison sentences at St. Lazare women's prison in May of 1890 when the second wave of the pandemic struck Paris. Her warden, Sister Léonide Lateuligne, belonged to the Sisters of Marie-Joseph, a Vincentian order responsible for the administration and day-to-day supervision of St. Lazare. Sr. Léonide considered Louise Michel an old familiar friend and had asked for her assistance in preparing the tent field hospital within the prison's central courtyard.

Louise Michel: The newspapers carry on as if their reporters are now medical doctors and scientists. They describe the most disgusting bodily functions while purporting to protect, as if doing us a *kindness*. Really. I prefer their mismanagement of the first wave of this *Asiatic grippe*, when they told us we had

---

[1] *The Evening World*, 1890

nothing to fear, to go about our business, and to recommence buying bread.

Parisians and their brioches!

Soeur Léonide: You must scoot that canvas over here, Lou-Lou. Please focus.

– I have not seen a brioche since this time last year. – When the *gendarmes* come, I want everything in position, so they do the heavy lifting as efficiently as possible.

Lou-Lou: As you wish, Bostock. Here, but it's heavy. You must help me roll it. You know, it's what *you* would call "a mercy" that my mother didn't live to see this plague. Is it my fault that they compare the lungs of sufferers to stale *petits pains* that harden and crumble... Were you sick with it in January?

Soeur Léonide: Two novices were spared; that's all. The rest of us were flattened as it picked off the elderly, five and ten at a time, and massacred the young working girls. Our novices were plunged into responsibility: nursing the sick, making funeral arrangements, corresponding with the Motherhouse for instructions, preparing the liturgies... When no one in the entire city could find a coffin to save his soul, the young ones wrote the family of each sister and discovered relatives who volunteered carpentry skills. So enterprising!

Lou-Lou: I don't know what to make of your nose for a bargain

---

[2] Frank Bostock, 1866-1912, famed lion tamer. When Sister Léonide lived and worked in the St. Lazare women's prison, the inmates there gave her the nickname, "Bostock."

while speaking of this scourge and its desecration. Is this any way for a nun to talk?

Soeur Léonide: You tease, but you're correct: it's no way to talk. Such devastation. Elsewhere, the young were spared, but here even the children received the worst that the plague could do; it's their poor diet, the cold damp that seeps into their bedding, the anger they hold inside that eats at their stomachs and spleens. When this invisible enemy swept in from Russia, our girls had no breath left to fight it.
– But Lou-Lou, you say I'd call it "a mercy" that your Maman has already kept her appointment with destiny. And you, sister? What would *you* call it?

Lou-Lou: Sister? Ha! I am not a sister as *you* are. But a sister all the same.
– Here, allow me to carry that basket of iron pegs. You are stronger than you look, but mine are the arms of a laborer in the field.

Léonide: My father is a stonemason. I often carried his iron tools for him. You cannot impress me with your muscles… And you forget that I'm aware of your aristocratic background. *Milady*.

Lou-Lou: Look at your sly smile, Bostock. You have won yet another round. Strange to say, though, your victories over me some-how feel like my own wins. Tell me, will we *really* carry the sick out here, to the courtyard? They'll grow damp before they reach their cots under the tents, and the air in this part of the city is a miasma. Will this not endanger those who are already suffering?

Léonide: The hallways and stairwells are no safer for them, and the

greater fear is for those not yet infected. Each day I send letters to the funeral homes. But no one has space for the corpses. The ice houses cannot keep pace with demand. This wave is more dangerous than the first, Lou-Lou.
– Also, I must remind you that you haven't said what word you prefer in place of "mercy."

Lou-Lou: I have not forgotten your question. All while you've been speaking, I've thought about how to answer. In truth, I do use the word *mercy*, but I am not comfortable using it in conversation with *you*. I know that you twist the meanings of words. You give them more weight until they're heavy things, too difficult to carry…

Léonide: Ah, you see? Another way in which my peasant strength is superior to yours!

Lou-Lou: My weakness, which you're quick to expose, does exist. You've uncovered it. Bravo, lion tamer.
Still, when I use words, I prefer that they soar across the page, skip along, and float over one another. Light words, words that travel well, words that lift people and inspire them. Words like falcons and crickets and singing beetles with diaphanous, iridescent wings…

Léonide: I don't wish to strip you of anything, dear Lou-Lou. And your words truly do attain the heights you wish for them.
– I'd only add that even words that lift and inspire can be "heavier" than you suspect.

Lou-Lou: Yes.
After the Commune, when they exiled me to New Caledonia, I tasted that distance between myself and my roots. I thought

I'd never see Maman again; my comrades had been butchered like pigs before my eyes. A heavy inspiration: the surprise that nothing at all of my life was mine to keep.

I see it in others, now: so many seem exiled from themselves, their happy habits, and companions who had once sat across the table... all evaporated. It is as if they lift a hand in front of their faces and do not recognize it. Isn't it so, Sister?

Léonide: I see what you see. But I meant something different, something not so sad.

Inspiration is richer, heavy – like cream.

For example: from the experiments of Dr. Pasteur, we know that the sickness is a small creature... It uses our bodies like trolley cars, jumping on, traveling for a time, then "switching trains" to infect the next person.

Lou-Lou: And?

Léonide: We each play host to the same "passenger," whom we *share*. And if we could climb into the sky, we would see that the trolley tracks form a single, interconnected design.

Lou-Lou: You are saying that the sense of exile is an illusion, that in fact the disease unites us ...

Léonide: The feeling of exile is part of the pattern traced by the rails.

Lou-Lou: But death, Bostock. Death isn't simply a decoration. She peels the rails from the earth, smashes trolley cars in merciless fists, and peels one track away from another, until all routes are impassible.

Léonide: We need to bring the basins and bedding. Will you please come with me to the storage attic?

Lou-Lou: Hah! I will never grow tired of your courteous manner when addressing a convict. *Bien,* I would be honored to accompany you...

Léonide: But Lou-Lou, do you think that in death all is lost? Forever?

Lou-Lou: Eh, no. Our bodies decompose; they nourish the pasture. Honeybees collect nectar from clover, and cows digest oat straw into milk –

Léonide: Don't forget the sparrows, who clean their feet in dew as they hop in the weeds –

Lou-Lou: – the same meadows produce seeds we crush into flour for our loaves –

Léonide: Then one day someone will bake *us* into brioches?

Lou-Lou: United, in a single, buttery brioche.

Léonide: You laugh, and I also find it funny. But in all honesty, Lou-Lou? This fate seems too *small.*

Lou-Lou: I admit to you: I find it dissatisfying...

Léonide: Here, let's stack the bedding under the tarp. The basins will keep best beside that sycamore.

Lou-Lou: I marvel at you. Every detail accounted for.
How many weeks did you administer the tent hospital in the prison exercise yard during the last wave?

Léonide: 37 long days. And every hour was like a year. During that time, 846 of our residents broke free…

Lou-Lou: And you really believe these convicts are "free" … *alive* and free?

Léonide: But why not? See here, Lou-Lou: words like "mercy" and "inspiration" contain depths …and substance –

Lou-Lou: And creaminess …

Léonide: Their very *heaviness* makes them rise – yes – as fat ascends to the top of the dairy pail.

Lou-Lou: Eh, but little Sister, if defeating mortality is simply a matter of fat content, then you are much better equipped for the resurrection than I am. You'd better start feeding your prisoners more butter if you wish to bring us with you to the great milk pasture in the sky!

Léonide: Your humor is another way to make words and meanings "fly," dear Lou-Lou.
   When you say it was "a mercy" that your mother did not live to experience this pestilence, what you really *mean* is that it was a sign of *love* that she was spared. Mercy and love are one and the same, and you love your Maman. Your love for her isn't confined to what you are able to achieve with your own strength and feeling. For this reason, if rain would drench her to the skin, you'd experience regret, as if you had been the one to permit this evil. You'd want to apologize for the cruel weather, though this would seem absurd to your logical mind. Despite your littleness and impotence in the matter, you'd rush to make amends for the downpour: with a towel you'd

rub warmth back into her limbs; then you'd bring her hot tea, or perhaps a glass of wine to restore color to her cheeks. Later, on a day when the clouds part and the afternoon sun caresses your Maman, you'd feel complicit in this light and bounty, too. You'd call it a "mercy," meaning that you intuit that the sun's magnanimity toward your mother was perhaps *caused* by your love for her… or at least this bounty has some share in your own desire for her happiness.

Lou-Lou: According to this reasoning, I would be to blame for her death. No?

Léonide: You'd *want* to blame yourself.

Lou-Lou: How would someone escape from such madness? Surely such an attitude could drag us to the very bottom of hell, with no escape.

Léonide: Human beings are resourceful. We invent diversions and use ordinary duties as distractions. We surround our work with so much anxiety and imaginary significance that we manage to forget death – almost. But death is there, like a sister. She takes one handle of the wheelbarrow and pushes alongside us as we cart the tent pegs and canvases.

Lou-Lou: Excuse me, but what about these trees, Sister? How will they survive under the tents?

Léonide: You'll see. The *gendarmes* are cunning. They configure the tarps so as not to obscure any branches. This also protects the sick from insects dropping on them.

Lou-Lou: I did not expect this illness to return for a second time. It is good that your Mother Superior saved the tent canvases and irons.

Léonide: She pays attention to mortality and often counsels us to contemplate our own passing. How many times has she said to me: *no one among the living can escape Sister Death's embrace?*

Lou-Lou: Forgive me, Bostock, but I must ask: when you entertain stories of an afterlife, aren't you using your imagination to create your own diversion?

Léonide: Alone, at night on my bed, I have often asked myself this question.

Lou-Lou: So… Your faith is … weak?

Léonide: You seem distressed at the thought! But I suspect that my faith, like yours, requires research and deep inquiry – in fact, a faith that stands up to interrogation is *strong*.

Lou-Lou: *Mine*?! My *faith*? I have no faith at all.

Léonide: You and I define this word differently. For you, it means a blind and irrational belief in ideas for which there can be no evidence or proof.

Lou-Lou: And for you…?

Léonide: Faith means being able to see the *whole* of everything, including invisible things like love, memory, and need. Without the eyes of faith, no one could perceive the pattern of historical events unfolding in the present. Most of all, faith sees meaning and traces connections between seemingly unrelated particulars.

Lou-Lou: According to this definition, my analysis of our cultural
　　　sickness – and really all investigations into the forces at work
　　　in history – would fall under the category of "faith." Surely
　　　this can*not* be how your bishops and superiors understand the
　　　word…

Léonide: Don't forget your certainty concerning the eventual
　　　triumph of Revolution –

Lou-Lou: The Revolution is not an imaginary realm in the sky.

Léonide: And where do you think the Kingdom may be found? It is
　　　made of your sweat, of the iron ore that turns my blood red,
　　　and of the sounds our words make now, as they leave our lips.
　　　The sky contains none of these elements… and yet it, too,
　　　offers a service that is *far* from imaginary. At any point, we
　　　can look up to find a document that measures the precise
　　　dimensions of our need and of the only species of love that
　　　can answer it.

Parking Mirror, Sharon Mollerus

Apocalypse
by Greg Huteson

If by the steps the old man, Flip,
a gnarled wisp with whiskered face,
his smoke tucked in arthritic grip,
and if he leans beneath a card
that lists a hefty smoking fine
and glares out at a latent yard,

And if he mumbles like a bear
then lifts his jaundiced eyes to God
or not to God but smoggy air
and starts to smoke and snubs the murk
while kids and fathers saunter by
and mothers race in cars to work…

The courtyard's quiet for the nonce
though vivid orchids drop their scraps
and long-tailed pigeons scout out haunts

to bide the humid heat, for dreams
and ecstasies of fallen fruit
that lodge somehow in hidden seams.

Then by the steps the wisp that's Flip
at long last thumps the butt with grace,
the tumbling scrap a smoky blip.
It settles on a square of yard,
soon starts an active, crackling blaze
that puts the neighbors on their guard.

They grouse then, shortly, shout their fears
and fling their blackened words at God.
Or not at God but cunning bears,
the burly ones who fight the flame
while dogs and kittens frolic on
and leopards lope in pairs, untame.

And the Needle Pulls
by Hannah Laurence

The sleeping artist weaves the strings
Considering their various stages
Of vibrancy and mutedness
Tension and docility
Together
Into a tapestry
Invisible to the natural eye
Leaving threads loose
On the side connected to the earth
And the needle pulls

Park Point, Dulth, Sharon Mollerus

What Baboons We Are!
by Hannah Laurence

What baboons we are!
We keep the best things secret and hang out the worst.

Holiday in Harlem
by Michial Farmer

I do wonder how many men
Who purchased her services
In those days of walking
The Manhattan streets,
Before she was
Billie, knew
That they were
Injecting her
With the suffering
She would one day breathe out,
As if through a tenor reed,
Always mixed with joy, light and dark
At once—a language only
She could speak, but one that
Everyone can read.
When they beat her,
Could they feel
Her spirit
Failing to crack,
Absorbing the pain,
Preparing to turn it
Into something ravishing,
Ephemeral and eternal?

Divestments
by Will Stenberg

First it was the belongings
I had to part with. The things
you gave to me.
Trinkets and tchotchkes now charged
with sorrow: I returned them
to your keeping.
But as the days passed, it was
my skin that bothered me. It
remembered you.
So I did what I always
do when I am in trouble:
went to the woods.
I found a yellow meadow,
the air a morning window,
and solemn as
a widow stepped out of my

skin. Skeletal I folded
it on the ground.
The wind began to speak with
the trees, the sun slipped behind
clouds. Not enough.
My heart. Of course. That great weight.
I removed it and with a
sharp rock, emptied
it out, set it on the ground
to be a den for something
small and lost. Wind
threaded my ribs and the night
bloomed. Still not enough. My lungs
that had inhaled
you I draped over a dark
branch for the crows. The rest of
my insides on
the ground for wolves. Now hollow
I did a little dance as
the moon chased the
sun from the sky and a night-
bird moaned a chorus that was
old when the world
was new. Not enough, nor close:
you were in my bones. So piece
by piece I took
myself apart, made a sad
mandala on the grass so
that, self-butchered,
there was nothing left of me.
A fawn entered my skin and
sweetly slept. The
snake looped in my heart's hollow

and hissed a psalm. The crows gorged,
the wolves left with
red snouts and the dawn came. The
sun emptied itself across
the meadow and
the dawn-birds took their shift. My
clean bones shone. In the hanging
moment before
the fall of day it remained,
an undying presence in
the air. The ache.

Window Seat, Sharon Mollerus

Glory in the Dead of Winter
by Jane Greer

Down into the valley I rise, screaming
alleluia along the bright and brittle air.
This is my weather: all I hear is my heart
as I climb the cold like falling into dreaming.
Coulees are rippled by a pulse of fear
as I pass overhead, my fleet art

the merest flick of shadow over snow.
This is my weather: I am unencumbered,
resting on this thermal above the butte,
by concepts such as yesterday, tomorrow,
now—while you, alas! your days are numbered.
My vision and my need are absolute.

This white basin of sky can never hold me;
soon I will spill over, I will change my cry,
plummet to do my existential damage.
To you it will seem to take an eternity—
or it will seem just a blink of your wet dark eye
in which is mirrored my inrushing image.

John the Baptist, Thomas Marsh

Eine Kleine Nachtmusik
by Jane Greer

Two of the homeschooled children from next door
pump the swings high and loudly *bum-bum-bum*
the Mozart they've been listening to. Before,
the golden hour was still, but for the hum
of locusts; now across the chokecherry border
of our yards, spilled through my green seclusion,
comes this bellowed order-in-disorder,
squeaky, crescendoing: a sudden fusion
of disparate pleasures into one delight,
here, for me, at this moment, on this night.

Parallelism (detail), Linnéa Gabriella Spransy

Louise Glück and the Return From Oblivion
by Ewa Chrusciel

You who do not remember
passage from the other world
I tell you I could speak again: whatever
returns from oblivion returns

to find a voice:
from the center of my life came
a great fountain, deep blue
shadows on azure seawater.
—Louise Glück

The recipient of the 2020 Nobel Prize in Literature, Louise Glück, is an erudite and contemplative poet comfortable in shuffling mythical, religious, mystical, and literary references. However, in a recent interview she shared a painful story of her inability to write for an extended period when she lived in Vermont. This story shed light on a struggle not only hers, but common to many writers. At that time, she could only read gardening catalogues. But there was one given line in her head that played over and over again: "At the end of my suffering there was a door."

Amidst these roadblocks she went to the garden and forced herself to write a poem about a flower. The next day she wrote another poem about another flower. On the third day, she knew what to do. And her collection *Wild Iris*, published in 1992 (and awarded the Pulitzer Prize), came to being in eight weeks. When she finished she had no memory of making it. It felt stolen. It felt like it came from someone else.

The book sounds like an act of recreating the world after coming back from a harrowing experience of darkness and depression. It reenacts the experience of grappling with faith. There are three distinguishable voices in the book: voices of flowers, the voice of a Gardener/poet, and the voice of the Divine (addressed sometimes as father or Father).

The titular "Wild Iris" introduces a polyvalence of references. It is written from the perspective of a wild iris and it alludes to the myth of return from death, reminiscent of Hades or the myth of Persephone. Literally speaking, a wildflower with consciousness and wisdom offers its perspective, but this same iris could also be read as the mythological daughter of the sea god Thaumas and an Oceanid, and sister of the Harpies. In the myth, Iris is a bridge between humans and Olympian gods, serving as a messenger. She is also the goddess of the rainbow that connects earth with the sky. She can travel as fast as the wind to both the bottom of the sea and the underworld.

In contrast with these mythological references, the next two poems, entitled "Matins," allude to the Catholic liturgical tradition of the Liturgy of the Hours practiced by clergy and the religious to sanctify each day. The Second Vatican Council revised the Liturgy of Hours into seven canonical hours, including matins and vespers. The hours rely heavily on psalms and have division of voices: there is antiphon 1 and 2—a voice that initiates and one that responds. Often when prayed by groups of people, chanting in two choirs is involved so the prayer is both dialogic and musical.

Analogical to the structure of Catholic Hours, Glück's book is comprised of seven poems called Matins and ten Vespers. In her lyric sequence, all voices (or personas) engage in conversations. Yet, the voices are not rigidly delineated but ambiguous, overlapping, and bleeding into each other. In the opening poem "Wild Iris" we read:

> *You who do not remember*
> *passage from the other world*
> *I tell you I could speak again: whatever*
> *returns from oblivion returns*
> *to find a voice...*

This poem could be read either as the voice of a wild iris or the voice of the poet.

The poem alludes to great suffering to the point of annihilation of the self. Departing from the underground of suffering, depression, or the dark night of the soul might also be a valid trope here. The next poem, "Matins," offers another reference to depression: "depressives hate the spring." Skipping one line, a speaking voice narrows the statement into: "being depressed, yes, but in a sense passionately/ attached to the living tree, my body/ actually curled in the split trunk, almost at peace/ in the evening rain/ almost able to feel/ sap frothing and rising." The poem suggests the trajectory from the dark night of the soul into romantic fusion with nature.

The next poem is reminiscent of Genesis and addressed to the unreachable father after the exile from heaven. The Greek word for exile, *xeniteia*, was meant originally for monks in antiquity—a detachment, going away to the desert to get closer to God. Analogically, the lyric sequence takes place in the earthly garden, after the exile from heaven. The trajectory is not linear, but circular, as these poems meander with recurring themes.

But overall we travel from the underworld of immense suffering to the natural world, and through the natural world to questioning and protesting the Infinite Mystery. Daniel Morris in *The Poetry of Louise Glück*, suggests that:

> The consistent but shifting format enables readers to chart a speaker's volatile emotional course—in the same way a photograph would if taken of the same person standing in the same place but at different times of the day and over several months.

These discursive, lyrical poems engage in constant conversation with an unknowable father, aiming at dialogue. God's voice also responds in several poems: "Spring Snow," "Retreating Wind," and "April," among others. Some poems such as "Witchgrass" are reminiscent of God responding to Job. As in Job's soliloquy, Glück's sequence is mournful, addressing loss, despair, nostalgia, immense suffering.

Monsignor Lorenzo Albacete, in *God at the Ritz*, claims that

IDS Center, Sharon Mollerus

suffering indicates the transcendence of the human person. He writes, "The suffering of human beings is a sign of God. What this God is like is another question." This sense of suffering as a sign of transcendence pervades Glück's poems. These poems never attempt to reduce or rationalize suffering, like Job's friends who try to explain away his loss. Rather, in Glück's poems, suffering indicates human transcendence by provoking the one who suffers to address God.

In this sense, these poems very much palpitate with the religious sense or even religious experience. Albacete defines religious experience as "a way of experiencing this world as a sign of a reality that is always beyond its limits." Accordingly, in Glück's poems, suffering is a religious experience in that it leads the one who suffers to look beyond the limits of the world and address herself to that beyond.

Similar to another Glück collection *Vita Nova*, there are also references to Dante's journey in *Wild Iris*. In the poem spoken by a trillium, a solitary three-petaled flower, we are reminded of Dante's famous opening of the *Inferno*. Glück writes, "When I woke up I was in a forest." There is a ladder in the poem "reaching through the firs," possibly a reference to Jacob's ladder (the sequence features a subsequent poem entitled "The Jacob's Ladder"—a wildflower but also a reference to Jacob's ladder in Genesis). Once again we have a transition from loss and darkness into heaven, possibly the moon and stars, as the poem takes place at night.

Giacomo Leopardi's "Night-Song Of A Wandering Shepherd of Asia (XXIII)" comes to mind:

> *Often as I gaze at you*
> *hanging so silently, above the empty plain*
> *that the sky confines with its far circuit:*
> *or see you steadily*
> *follow me and my flock:*
> *or when I look at the stars blazing in the sky,*
> *musing I say to myself:*

"What are these sparks,
this infinite air, this deep
infinite clarity? What does this
vast solitude mean? And what am I?"

Like flowers that are dependent on a gardener, the Gardener-Poet in the poems also seeks transcendent dependence. However, the Mystery is indiscernible and unknowable in Glück's lyrical sequence. At first, the voice of the Gardener addresses God as "unreachable father." In the next "Matins," God is portrayed as "unconceivable" via human imagination.

Forgive me if I say I love you: the powerful
are always lied to since the weak always
driven by panic.
I cannot love
what I can't conceive, and you disclose
virtually nothing: are you like the hawthorn tree,
always the same thing in the same place,
or are you more the foxglove, inconsistent, first springing up
a pink spike on the slope behind the daisies,
and the next year, purple in the rose garden? You must see
it is useless to us, this silence that promotes belief
you must be all things, the foxglove and the hawthorn tree,
the vulnerable rose and tough daisy—we are left to think
you couldn't possibly exist. Is this
what you mean us to think, does this explain
the silence of the morning,
the crickets not yet rubbing their wings, the cats
not fighting in the yard?

Is God in the above poem presented as a cloud of unknowing, or is this Yahweh whose name was revealed to Moses as four Hebrew consonants and whose pronunciation was forbidden in the Jewish tradition? God reveals himself to Moses as He Who Brings into Existence Whatever Exists. He is beyond comprehension and description. Furthermore, St Paul's "Aeropagus Speech" in Acts 17:23 comes to mind in which he praises Greeks for their religiosity and mentions an altar "To An Unknown God" the Athenians worshipped. In his sermon Paul specifies further this unknown, foreign God:

> He made from one blood every nation of men to dwell on all the surface of the earth, having determined appointed seasons, and the boundaries of their dwellings, that they should seek the Lord, if perhaps they might reach out for him and find him, though he is not far from each one of us.

Glück intuits both the nearness and inscrutability of the unknown God, as well as the frustration resulting from the inability to "pinpoint" the Mystery of God.

In the following poem, in response to one discussed above, the voice of the Gardener rebukes herself for speaking to Infinity in a personal way. The mystery seems remote, absent. Yet the speaker's agnosticism is punctured with a desire for a human, personal God.

The next poem, spoken by Scilla—a collective flower that spreads in waves and offers the best blues—is yet another counter-response to the desire for an individual relationship with God: "Not I, you idiot, not self, but we, we—waves/of sky blue like/a critique of heaven," says Scilla to the Gardener.

Somewhere in the middle of the book there is a shift from lowercase father to capital Father. A Matins sequence starts as an accusation, a protest, and transitions to a prayer:

> *I am the lowest of your creatures, following*
> *The thriving aphid and the trailing rose—Father,*

as agent of my solitude, alleviate
at least my guilt; lift
the stigma of isolation, unless
it is your plan to make me
sound forever again . . .
In counter-response, field flowers, acting as naysayers, respond by
cynically provoking doubt again:
What are you saying? That you want
eternal life?
[...]
O
the soul! the soul! Is it enough
only to look inward?

Perhaps the flowers could be understood as splintered identities of a wounded self, and the whole sequence a dramatic monologue. I concur with Daniel Morris, who in *The Poetry of Louise Glück*, proposes that "The tonal similarity of these voices suggests that the dialogism of these grouped lyrics is really a foil for an internal conversation."

The voice seems to waver and mature and waver again. The religious sense shifts from questioning to wonder in the next "Matins":

I am ashamed
at what I thought you were,
distant from us, regarding us
as an experiment...
Dear friend,
Dear trembling partner, what
surprises you most in what you feel,
earth's radiance or your own delight?
For me, always,
The delight is the surprise.

From Matins we move towards Vespers as a transition from morning questioning and doubt, to evening maturation and a more intimate, personal relationship with God. The first "Vespers" sounds almost like intimate teasing of God: perhaps you exist but in warmer climates where fig trees grow. "Perhaps they see your face in Sicily; here we barely see the hem of your garment." The complaint directed to God is much more tender, intimate than at the beginning of the sequence: "And no one praises more intensely than I, with more/ painfully checked desire."

The tenderness also manifests itself as humor in conversation with the Divine in a Vespers poem reminiscent of one of Christ's parables of a vineyard:

> *In your extended absence, you permit me*
> *use of earth, anticipating*
> *some return or investment. I must report*
> *failure in my assignment, principally*
> *regarding the tomato plants.*

Yet another significant transition takes place in recognizing God in the human being, hence intuiting incarnation. God descends into human flesh, becomes one of us.

> *I don't wonder where you are anymore*
> *You're in the garden; you are where John is,*
> *In the dirt, abstracted, holding his green trowel.*

The whole sequence takes the shape of a love affair between creation and a Creator. When human desire is exhausted, it reaches beyond; it transcends.

> *why would you wound me, why would you want me*
> *desolate in the end, unless you wanted me so starved for hope*

> *I would refuse to see that finally*
> *nothing was left to me, and would believe instead*
> *in the end you were left to me.*

In "Lullaby," the lover, God, responds to his beloved with affection and tenderness:

> *Time to rest now; you have had*
> *enough excitement for the time being.*
> *[...]*
> *Don't think of these things anymore.*
> *Listen to my breathing, your own breathing*
> *like the fireflies, each small breath*
> *a flare in which the world appears.*
> *I've sung to you long enough in the summer night.*
> *I'll win you over in the end; the world can't give you*
> *this sustained vision.*
> *You must be taught to love me. Humans being must be*
> *taught to love*
> *silence and darkness.*

The overall sequence is an intimate conversation with God, which becomes—in its meanderings and storming of the walls of mystery—a twisted journey of an apophatic via negativa that in the end leads to the light and the maturation of the relationship between the child and the Father.

Wild Iris is an act of recreating the world, and the suffering in that birthing is palpable. It also is a testament to the hope that at the end of each suffering there is a door. It is a reminder that our own creations are not just the product of our will; that just like a flower depends on a seed, a gardener, so too a gardener depends on the Gardener. The book helps to intuit that it is not through our efforts that we receive grace. We must unearth that gift, a treasure. It is like a seed whose flower comes from someone else beyond the gardener or the soil.

The Peace That Hides
by Andrew Calis

Still, *Shantih* haunts me in my sleep.
Like the afterlife—clichéd in golden light,
or else a sentence kept somewhere—the deep
of truth like matter, in shapes that we can't know.

I rest in that uncertainty sometimes,
almost passing out, waking right
before I see past the veil, the lines
just starting to *mean*, the early glow
of morning. To know the maker's heart—that
would be something. But it wouldn't be
peace. Just knowledge, that long-forgotten Tree,
deep-rooted in my want. The broken back
that labor curved, and the human need for rest:
It noses at me like
some tired thing; it curls within my chest,
or else I feel the first sharp stings of its bite—

And I am no more found than when we were cast
out of the garden, guilty, staring back
and seeing the fires glowing like light at last.

The Voices in the Wind
by Andrew Calis

I.   Home

My father, forty years ago, came
across the sea with just enough to eat.
He spoke; was silenced. Spoke again; was thought
an imbecile, an animal, a stain.
(He recalls this to us, on shifting feet.)
My freedom wasn't bought
by me; it isn't something I could
have bought. His sacrifice was a higher
calling, a vocation—a close-held pain.
His history weighs on his tongue like wood.
He waits, will kindle his dried heart into a fire.

II.   Heaven

The raging fire, the ground that, thundering, shook
the mountaintop, the wind that in its great breath
bent the trees in two, Elijah heard.
But these were not the instruments of God.
No. In the silence of the breeze,
God spoke. He made the heart, he must
have spoken life. He must have shaken off the dust
of death and spread far-fingered roots,
the love-veined roots that tie us to the Earth
and to each other, the humanness that birthed us,
all alike at birth—vulnerable
and broken. Until we're seen
with those first eyes, that deep
unspoken look, the tears that shatter light;
the arms that guard the smallness of ourselves;
the arms that keep us close to love as touch
until we're consumed, surrounded by the largeness
of the act, the warmth that grows and grows
beyond its rim, the overwhelming fire of love.

Artist Statement
by Linnéa Gabriella Spransy

Using strict rules, I construct images on the belief that limits have an eerie capacity to generate surprise...even freedom. Chaos and emergent system theory tell us that these limits need not be elaborate, or even obviously visible; in fact, it is often the most humble and self-evident limits, which, in time, behave in the most sophisticated ways. They form bizarre chandeliers of crystal, guide the catacomb construction of ant colonies, the spread of cities, and the swoop of flocks, all, often, with eerie similarity. Awareness of these limits does not guarantee predictive power, or the ennui of omniscience.

This is good, and fascinating.

And it is through this means that I make my work: every piece is the manifestation of a predetermined scheme – a system of small limits with a clear beginning and end. Using abstract symbol (what I call "modules," much like number and letter forms) in a mode of familiar, naturalistic construction, these pieces of visual script are allowed to accrue and to display their peculiar surprises. In this way, an unlikely path of discovery is opened in the midst of certainty- though every step is predetermined and the end known from the beginning, the final form remains enigmatic. Though I have accumulated an extensive archive of "research drawings," end results are stubbornly, delightfully immune to absolute prediction.

Add to these systems environmental pressures (in this case, cataclysmic spills of paint flung over fully realized systems) and the flexibility and regenerative capacity of a given set of rules is tested even further. The system must then respond and rebuild using fragments of surviving information. Images generated this way hover near familiarity but are unable to declare themselves. They occupy both the micro and macroscopic view. They are both geologically slow and disastrously swift.

Working this way, I have become convinced that intelligence can be essentially understood as the ability to create or recognize pattern; perhaps patterns themselves are a form of intelligence – intelligence capable of surprise, without breaking a single rule. Which, in the end, is a satisfying contradiction, an energetic tension of philosophical forces hospitable to constrained freedom and consistent astonishment.

Recompositions of Sonnets to Michelangelo by Vittoria Colonna (No. 4, 19, 31, 41)

by Anna Key

No. 4

Abyss of true light, immense and pure, you
turn your kind and loving eyes toward us, we
who crawl about the world like ants, not free
but worldly-wise and hard of heart. Undo
the hurtful wall of ignorance that grew
like the lengthening shadow, cold and darkly,
of the old Adam—impious enemy
of your warm rays, clear and sure and new.
O God my God, clothe us with living faith and
loving fire; fold your law into our hearts like
leaven; teach us to fly, to leave behind
selfish desire, caught in itself like a lake.
Beyond it, where we lightly go, your hand
hands us the key your sweet gates to unlock.

No. 19

Your gift, Lord, is that a mortal being
can attain the infinite; you came down
to die our death that we, wearing your crown,
might share your life. The cross is the door. Seeing
you hanging there, hanging and not fleeing,
though you could, not seeing I would surely drown
in the desperately confused brown
waters of a despairing finitude. Freeing
us from that uncertain sea was a gift
that none could comprehend, but many have
forgotten. Too familiar now, we lay
claim to our finitude and try to lift
ourselves on wings of our own making, heaving
ourselves into a mute sky made of clay.

No. 31

If the faint sound, which alone stirs and moves
the frail air, stirs and moves me; and the breeze
gathers up the pieces of me, gently, and frees
my mind from the world's seductive grooves
to say in a weak whisper, *Love proves*
itself in weakness; if I am seized
with love for you when I hear you in the trees
and fall to my knees alone, all other loves
being gone; what then will my weak heart do
when my inner ear hears your soft voice spoken
in the quiet music of the sky, which told
and still tells of a world wholly true
where the steady rhythm is never broken
and the heavenly sound never grows old?

No. 41

What am I holding onto, that I should be
so sad? is maybe what he thought leaning
his head upon the breast of our Lord. Meaning,
perhaps, that time seen through is still and only
time, horizon of hurt, betrayal, friendly
fire, of things that go wrong, or seem to; weaning
ourselves off of its comforts and cleaning
the dirty panes of its desires lets us see,
if only a little, beyond the despair
of now. But still things end, painfully, and
goodbyes are still, if not forever, hard
to say; he felt it all, and felt it hard to bear,
and felt in his soul what he couldn't understand;
then gave us the Prologue as our eternal guard.

Solar Blush (detail), Linnéa Gabriella Spransy

A Larger Suit of Will
by Elisabeth Kramp

In enterprise the all–sided sword beams
emblematic, a larger suit of will every beyond
reach please reach to practice one joy.

Peace must be a place unimpeachable,
a place I will go and not alone.
The cool coil of it in the body

radiates in its fragile durability whole
that larger suit of will ever beyond reach
by which we practice what we can of peace.

If anger's our dogma, how undoing,
inscribing into flesh edicts against love.
As precious as peace—the will for peace to grow.

Contributors

Andrew Calis is a poet, teacher, and husband, and an overjoyed father of four. His first book of poetry, *Pilgrimages* (Wipf & Stock, 2020), was praised by James Matthew Wilson for having "the intensity of Hopkins" and for "layer[ing] light on light in hopes of helping us to see." His work has appeared in *America: The Jesuit Review, Dappled Things, Presence, Convivium*, and elsewhere. He teaches at Archbishop Spalding High School in Maryland.

Ewa Chrusciel is a bilingual poet and translator whose books in English include *Contraband of Hoopoe* (Omnidawn Press, 2014), *Of Annunciations* (Omnidawn, 2017), and *Strata* (2011). Included in her many Polish translations are Jack London's *White Fang* and Joseph Conrad's *The Shadow-Line*.

Fred Dale is a husband to his wife, Valerie, and a father to his occasionally good dog, Earl. He is a faculty member in the Department of English at the University of North Florida. He earned an MFA from the University of Tampa, but mostly, he just grades papers. His work has appeared in *Sugar House Review, The Summerset Review, Chiron Review, Tipton Poetry Journal*, and *The Evansville Review*, and his poems have twice been nominated for a Pushcart Prize.

Pellegrine Deuel devotes the better part of each day to wondering about the distinction between fiction and history and the connection between signs and what they reveal, fomenting revolution, and dispensing relationship advice.

Michial Farmer is the author of *Imagination and Idealism in John Updike's Fiction* (Camden House, 2017) and the translator of Gabriel Marcel's *Thirst* (Cluny Media, 2021). His poems have appeared in *Relief, The Blue Nib*, and *Eunoia Review*. He lives in Atlanta.

Mary Margaret Freeman's poetry has appeared in *The Christian*

Century, First Things, Outside the Lines, Poets Reading the News, The Hillsdale Review, and the *Catholic Poetry Room*. In 2017, she presented her long poem, "The Climbing Tree," before a live audience at Scratch: Works-in-Progress at Living Arts of Tulsa. In 2015, she won second place for "Storm Headaches" for adult poetry in the Tulsa City-County Library creative writing competition. In her work, she explores the contradictions inherent in creation, faith, and human and divine love. She currently lives in Tulsa, Oklahoma.

Jane Greer founded and edited *Plains Poetry Journal* (1981-1993), a literary magazine that was an advance guard of the New Formalism movement. Her poetry collections are *Bathsheba on the Third Day* (The Cummington Press, 1986) and *Love like a Conflagration* (Lambing Press, 2020). She was out of the poetry world for three decades but re-entered recently; since then, she's enjoyed publication in and acceptances by journals such as *First Things, National Review, Modern Age, Literary Matters*, and *The St. Austin Review*.

Greg Huteson's poems have appeared in or are forthcoming from *The Christian Century, Saint Katherine Review, Better Than Starbucks, The Road Not Taken*, and other journals. For the past twenty years he's lived in China and Taiwan, and his writing often reflects these contexts.

Anna Key has published poetry and criticism at *Dappled Things* and elsewhere. She lives with her husband and four children on an engineless sailboat, where they create videos about the poetry of life on the water at *Sailing Blowin' in the Wind* [YouTube channel].

Elisabeth Kramp lives in Southern California with her family. Her chapbook *Quickening* was published by Franciscan University Press, and her poems have been published in *First Things, Literary Matters*, and elsewhere. She teaches writing courses at John Paul **the** Great Catholic University and enjoys her work and play with her three young sons.

Hannah Laurence writes poetry from her home in San Diego and shares it at *outoftheprose.com*. Inspired and interrupted by her two young children and young-at-heart partner, she distills verse out of the prose of each day, wrestling with themes of motherhood, womanhood, spirituality, and shame.

Sharon Mollerus lives in Duluth, Minnesota, where she works as a social media and education assistant at the Tweed Museum of Art. She is an avid amateur photographer, with a special interest in museum, travel, and nature shots. She also sings with the choir of the Cathedral of Our Lady of the Rosary.

Will Stenberg is a poet, screenwriter, and musician who grew up in the wilds of Northern California and currently lives in Portland, Oregon, with his dog, Marlowe, and his box turtle, Scully.

Linnéa Gabriella Spransy holds an M.F.A. from Yale University School of Art and a B.F.A. in Drawing from the Milwaukee Institute of Art and Design. More of Linnéa's work can be seen on her website: *https://linneagabriella.com*.

Convivium is grateful for the support of its friends, and we appreciate your encouragement and your submissions.

We also appreciate your tax-deductible contributions, which can be sent to: Revolution of Tenderness
117 South Hollywood Blvd. #12
Steubenville, OH 43952
http://www.revolutionoftenderness.net

For more information about our work, please contact Suzanne Lewis at:
suzanne@revolutionoftenderness.net.

CPSIA information can be obtained
at www.ICGtesting.com
Printed in the USA
BVHW080021160222
629079BV00008B/825